Netallie and Eitan, you are the heart of
my **creativity** and **inspiration**.

Yaron, your abundant **support** allowed
me to cross the finish line.

For Eli,
Grow up BRAVE &
UNAFRAID!

Fondly,

Arielle Turover Cohen

I Am Brave and Unafraid

For more information, please contact:
Mascot Books
620 Herndon Parkway, Suite 320
Herndon, VA 20170
info@mascotbooks.com
www.mascotbooks.com

Library of Congress Control Number: 2017914712

CPSIA Code: PRT0118A
ISBN-13: 978-1-68401-379-1

Printed in the United States

I Am Brave and Unafraid

Written by
Arielle Turover Cohen

Illustrated by
Ignacio G.

MB®

Once upon a biscuit there was a little boy.

The boy loved camping. He put on his backpack, grabbed his teddy bear, Marshmallow, and kissed his mommy, daddy, and sister goodbye.

Then he wandered into the woods.

The boy reached his
most special camping
spot, set up his tent,
and built a fire.

He roasted a marshmallow until it was
big, puffy, and golden brown.

Then, he ate it all up.

The boy sat back
in his chair, licked
his fingers, and
joyfully sang...

I am out here in the woods, all alone,
I didn't even bring my telephone.
I love to see the stars, the sky, the moon,
I love to softly sing my little tune.

The boy gazed up at the twinkling stars and found Orion's Belt, his very favorite constellation.

He stood up tall like Orion the Hunter. He drew back his bow and arrow and shouted,

"Release!!!"

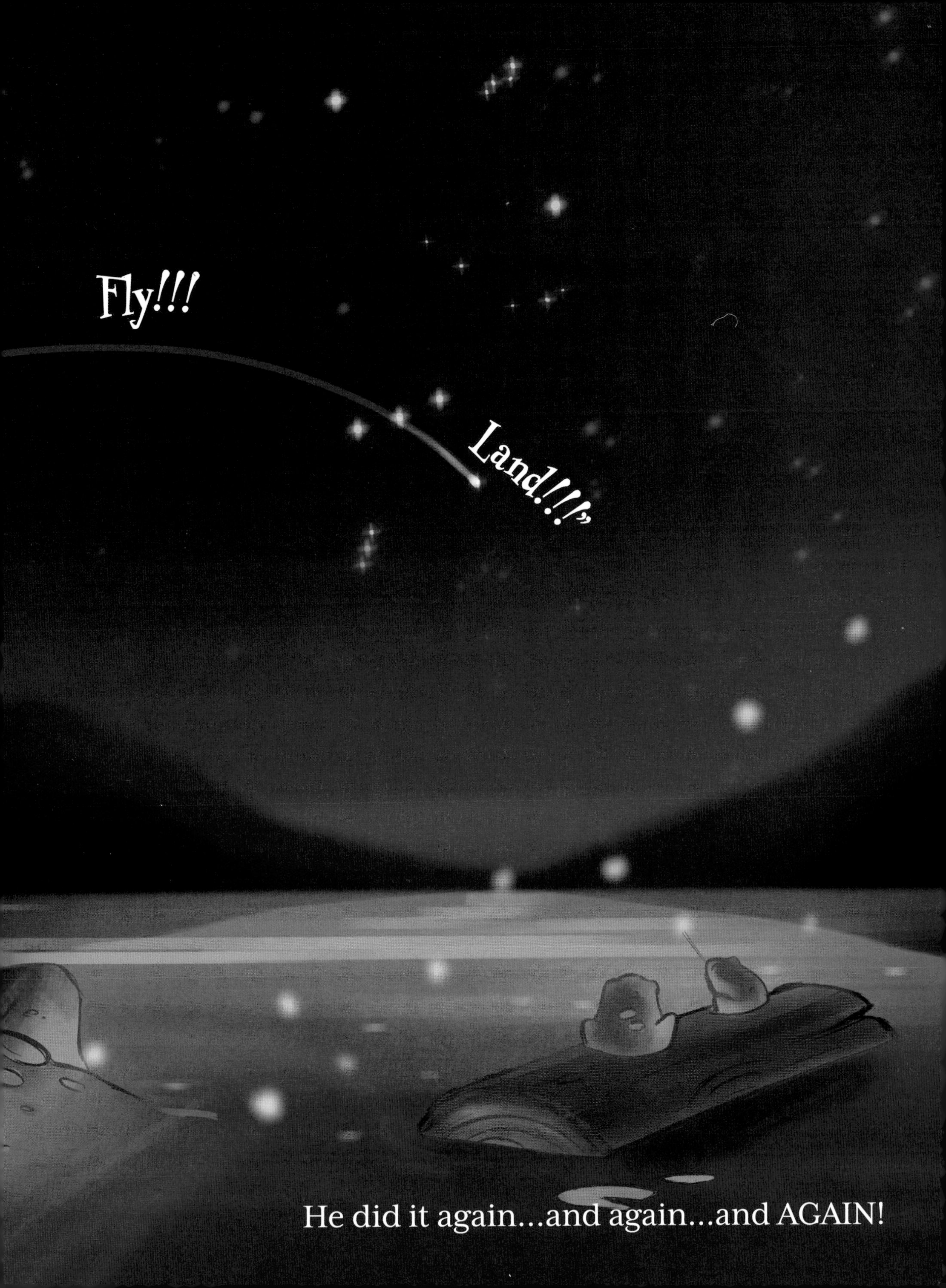

He did it again…and again…and AGAIN!

Eventually, the boy
yawned loudly,
rubbed his eyes, and
headed off to bed.

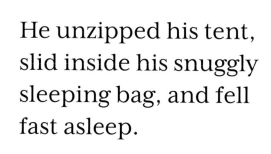

He unzipped his tent,
slid inside his snuggly
sleeping bag, and fell
fast asleep.

As he was sleeping he heard…

RRROAARRRI

The boy pulled the sleeping bag up over his head and shook.

What was that noise?

Was it a lion? NO*!!!!*

Was it a tiger? NO*!!!!*

Was it a B-B-B-B-BEAR???

Is a **BEAR** out there?

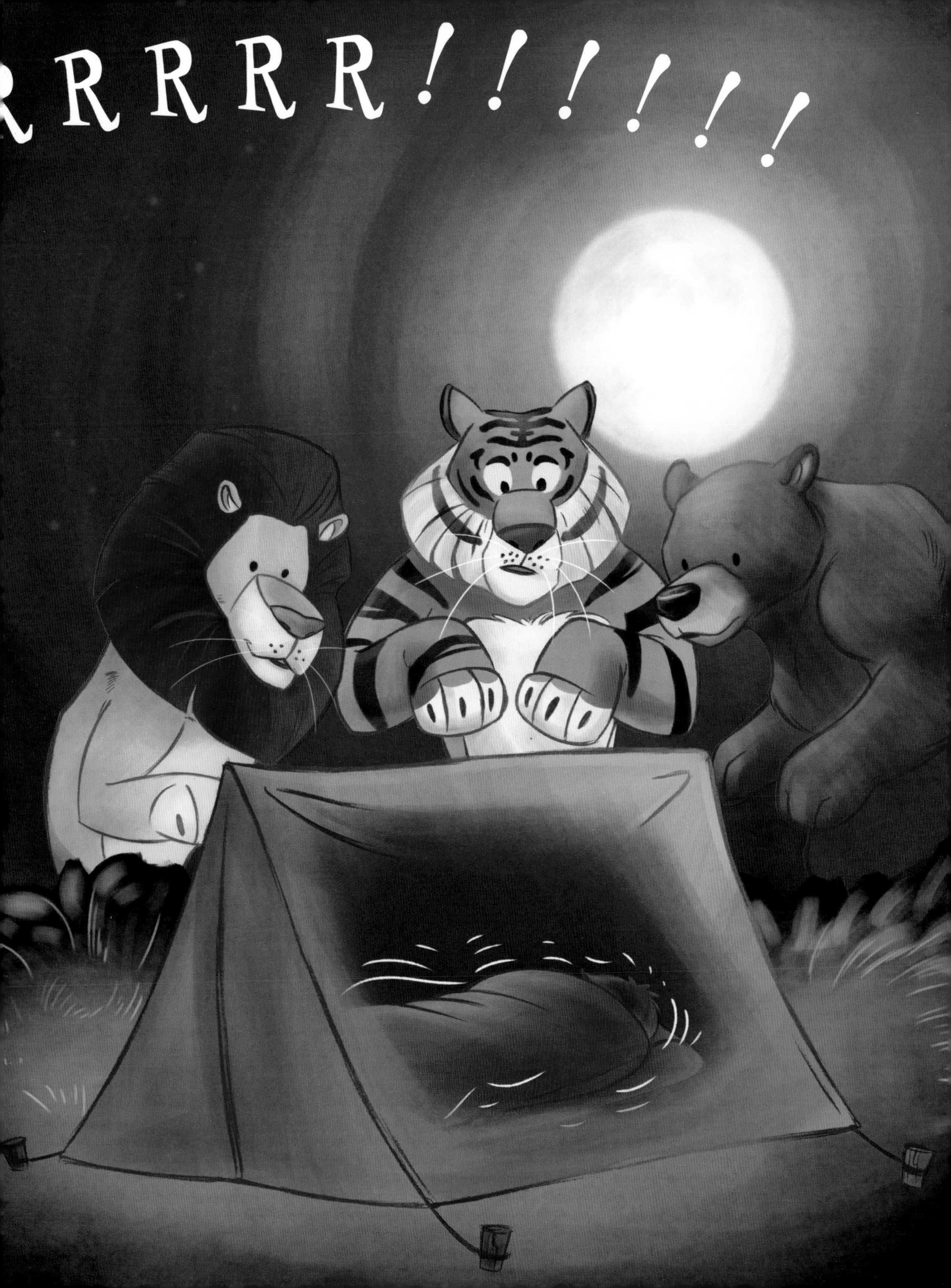
RRRRR!!!!!!

He took a deep breath in...
and slowly exhaled out...

The boy peeked through the
slit of his sleeping bag.

He looked left.

He looked right.

He didn't see anything, so he
sang himself back to sleep.

I am out here in the woods, all alone,
I didn't even bring my telephone.
I love to see the stars, the sky, the moon,
I love to softly sing my little tune.

As he was sleeping he heard...

RRROAARRRR

The boy pulled the sleeping bag up over his head and stayed as still as possible.

What was that noise?

Was it a lion? NO!!!!

Was it a tiger? NO!!!!

Was it a B-B-B-B-BEAR???

Is a BEAR out there?

He silently counted.

One…

two…

three…

The boy peeked through the slit of his sleeping bag. He listened.

He heard the wind.

WHOOOSHHHH

He heard the frogs.

CROOOAAAKK

He didn't hear anything else, so he sang himself back to sleep.

I am out here in the woods, all alone,
I didn't even bring my telephone.
I love to see the stars, the sky, the moon,
I love to softly sing my little tune.

As he was sleeping he heard...

RRROAARRRF

The boy pulled the sleeping bag up over his head and imagined he was invisible.

What was that noise?

Was it a lion? NO*!!!!*

Was it a tiger? NO*!!!!*

Was it a B-B-B-B-BEAR???

Is a BEAR out there?

He thought and thought about
what to do next.

The boy peeked through the
slit of his sleeping bag.

He saw a large shadow moving outside his tent.
The boy courageously repeated to himself...

I am brave and unafraid.

"I am brave and unafraid.

I am BRAVE and UNAFRAID!"

The boy bravely stepped
out of his sleeping bag,
confidently unzipped his tent,

and stood face to face with...

his big puffy golden brown
Marshmallow!

The boy rubbed his eyes,

looked down at
Marshmallow,
and snuggled
him tightly.

The boy yawned
a big yawn,
closed his eyes,

and fell fast asleep, smiling.

A Little Tune

I am out here in the woods, all a-lone, I did-n't ev-en bring my tel- e- phone. I

love to see the stars, the sky, the moon. I love to soft-ly sing my li- ttle tune.

About the Author

Arielle Turover Cohen has a passion for helping others embrace an *I Can* attitude. She believes that her book, *I Am Brave and Unafraid,* will inspire your child to build the courage to overcome challenges. In addition to writing, Arielle spends her time with her family, practices real estate, and hangs out in various yoga poses. She lives with her husband and two children in Berwyn, Illinois.

About the Illustrator

Ignacio G. has a love for animation which got him interested in art at age five. He studied at Laguna College of Art and Design, and now pursues his dream of illustrating children's books. He lives with his cats in Washington.

www.iambraveandunafraid.com